Going All In

A 1Night Stand Story

By
Lily Vega

Copyright © 2016 by Lily Vega
ISBN: 978-1-68361-019-9
Cover art by Renee Rocco

Published by Decadent Publishing Company, LLC
Look for us online at:
www.decadentpublishing.com

Dear Readers,

Have you considered chucking it all and running off to a fantasy world?

When I'm not escaping into a book I'm writing or reading, Las Vegas is my favorite place to do just that. I've played Texas Hold 'em in many poker rooms both on and off the Strip. Most times, I'm not the only woman at the table. I've played in tournaments and cash games. I've won and I've lost. I've relished the feeling of scooping up a pot and tipping the dealer. I've had the nuts and I've bluffed. I've read tells and displayed my own. I've dreamed of playing in the Ladies' event of the World Series of Poker.

Going All In is my love poem to the game of poker. I hope this story inspires you to take a chance and go all in to follow a dream or try something new. Win or lose, you'll be enriched by the experience.

Cheers!

Lily Vega

@LV_Writer
www.lilyvega.com
LilyVegaWriter@Gmail.com

Dedication

Going All In is for the hardworking casino employees who make Las Vegas my favorite travel destination. Big thanks to Kerry Adrienne, Louisa Bacio, Amelia Calhan, Anna Campbell, Rachel Firasek, Kelly Lynne, Kenzie Mack, Valerie Mann, and the Moonshine Critique Group.

Chapter One

I an Harding's heart slammed in his chest in time with the boom-boom-boom bass of the song playing over the poker room's sound system. Jittery from too much casino coffee and too many crappy cards, he prayed for a considerable win. Life had sucker-punched him in the gut with a side kick to the balls. And the majority of his escape fund lay in the mound of chips in the center of the poker table, out of reach and in jeopardy.

Slot machines screamed for attention, and patrons from the nearby sports book cried out in joy or sorrow at every football touchdown, field goal, and flag. He blocked out the casino activity around him and concentrated on the bounty of chips at stake in this game of Texas Hold 'Em.

The dealer revealed the river, the king of hearts.

Ian struggled to keep a neutral expression. Lady Luck finally favored him. The pair of kings in his hand with the king and pair of twos on the board gave him a full house. A boat. A winner-winner, chicken dinner. His empty stomach made a garbage-disposal gurgle at the thought of food. *How long has it been since my last decent meal?*

Fighting back from an epic losing streak, he'd managed to rebuild his diminishing chip stack with the last bill in his wallet. If he failed to win a big hand, he'd be forced to return to the pawnshop to trade in his few remaining possessions for cash. In front of him, his hole cards begged him to take another peek at their regal portraits, and his fingers itched to lift them from the scratchy table felt. Instead, he laced them together on his lap and willed his hands to stop shaking.

The dealer nodded toward the only other player at the table who hadn't folded, a man sporting a comb-over and the sleazy vibe of a corrupt politician fresh from a stint in a low-security penitentiary. "The action is to you, Mr. Richards."

Having bet heavily on the turn, the man tapped the felt indicating a check then snapped his fingers at the cocktail waitress and pointed to his glass, empty except for melting ice.

The waitress bewitched Ian with her wavy, dark-brown hair, sparkling-green eyes, and killer curves. Whenever she walked by the table, his thoughts drifted from the game. Something about her captivated him. Maybe how she tugged at her miniskirt when she thought no one watched. Or the way she greeted each of the local players by name. Or perhaps because too damned much time had passed since he'd spent an evening with a beautiful woman rather than a computer screen filled with numbers. He longed to invite her to dinner in the casino coffee shop, but he'd come to Vegas to escape his problems. He couldn't afford the distraction a bewitching brunette would bring.

"I'll be right back to take your order." Her shoulders slumped as though she carried a strongbox of sorrow in addition to a full tray of glassware and bottles.

"Do your job and get my drink. Scotch on the

rocks. Top shelf. Not that cheap shit you brought last time." The player smirked at the man sitting next to him. "With a rack like that, she doesn't need a high IQ."

A scarlet flush crept up the woman's neck, and her left eye twitched. She spun away and walked briskly in the direction of the bar.

Mr. Richards couldn't be more of a dick.

The dealer nodded at Ian. The brushfire of his hunger pains faded, replaced by an inferno of anger. His mission shifted from winning enough money to buy dinner, to wiping Dick's face clean of his pompous leer.

"All in." Ian pushed his remaining chips forward. In his haste, he shoved along the voucher he'd won earlier in the day in a casino promotion. Anxious to get to the poker room, he hadn't examined it.

"Keep your coupon. You're gonna need it." Dick flicked the paper toward him. "I call."

Ian revealed the kings and waited, hands outstretched, to receive his winnings. *Maybe I'll spring for a beer with my steak.*

The dealer examined both upturned hands and

pushed the pile of chips toward Dick.

Ian couldn't wrap his mind around the pairs of twos.

"Never seen quad deuces before, boy?" The jackass arranged the chips in teetering towers.

A Mack truck drove its oversized tires over Ian's heart, shifted into reverse, and crushed his ribcage a second time. The asshole had made four deuces. Ian estimated the odds of that hand to be a little more than 0.8 percent.

Shit. Shit. Shit.

"Where the hell is that bimbo with my drink?" Dick took a pull on his cigar. The cloud of smoke he blew out hung over the table in an ominous fog.

The word, *bimbo,* spiked Ian's adrenaline. He pushed back his chair, jarring the waitress standing behind him.

Brown liquid splashed across Dick's shirt. "Stupid slut." He tossed a dollar chip over his shoulder. "That's it, bend over and pick it up. I'm sure you spend plenty of time on your knees."

Ian retrieved the chip, placed it on her tray, and glared at Dick. "Don't be an ass. Everyone deserves respect."

The guy sneered. "The cash station is next to the buffet. If you want respect, come back and earn it."

Ian stood and poked his chest. "You should apologize."

"Floor." Dick shouted above the sound of poker chips and player chatter.

The poker room manager, a muscled hulk who could have moonlighted as a bouncer or a World Wrestling Federation Intercontinental Champion, rushed to his side.

Dick gestured at Ian. "This man is disturbing me."

"If you leave quietly, I won't call security." The manager led Ian out of the poker room. Once out of Dick's earshot, he whispered, "I'm really sorry, but Mr. Richards is a high roller."

The constant clang of slot machines gave the impression winners filled the casino, but Ian knew the truth. Risking all of his money in an attempt to teach the idiot a lesson had made him a loser. To win, he needed to keep his emotions at bay. He should have walked away after losing his initial buy-in. But, no matter how far he got from Portland, he couldn't seem to stop his mistakes from compounding.

"Excuse me." A lilting female voice drew him away from his mental self-flagellation.

The waitress. His dream woman. The Enchantress.

"Thanks for standing up for me." She held out a slip of paper. "You forgot this at the table."

Her hourglass figure filled out her uniform of a red corset and black miniskirt. He dragged his eyes from her cleavage and accepted the voucher. He wouldn't be like Dick and ogle her.

"Thank you."

The deodorant body spray he'd doused himself with after waking did little to disguise his need for a shower. If only they could've met under different circumstances. His face itched under her scrutiny, and he scratched his beard stubble.

Her eyes sparkled, and her lips curved into a smile. The kind of smile displayed by gamblers in the sports book when their horse crossed the finish line and they held the winning ticket. She handed him a bottle of water from her tray.

He reached into his pocket for a tip but found only lint. Once he returned from the pawnshop, he'd find her and give her a gratuity.

Ignoring his open palm, she kept her eyes locked on his. "Have a nice evening." With a sway of her hips, she walked away.

Ian flipped the paper over. The voucher provided an email address and offer for a complimentary date arranged by a Madame Evangeline and her online dating service, 1Night Stand.

A good fuck would relieve his tension. On the other hand, a sandwich and a decent night's sleep would be a better bet. He couldn't stand another overnighter in his car. Constant folding of his six-foot-two-inch frame into a semi-horizontal position in the sports coupe had mangled his spine. If he ever had the guts to return to his old life in Portland, he'd spend some quality time with a chiropractor.

Draining the bottle of water, he averted his gaze from a sign advertising the $9.99 steak dinner. He didn't have enough money for a cup of coffee, let alone a hot meal. At least his cell phone service hadn't been cut off yet. He punched out a quick email to Madame Evangeline on the tiny keyboard and headed for the food court where the employees handed out samples speared on toothpicks. The voucher and the free food would buy him a few more hours before he would need to return to the tables and pray for his luck to return.

He tucked his phone into his pocket and his gold and emerald University of Oregon class ring caught the light. Once he took the ring to the pawnshop, his last chance to make good would be on the table.

Chapter Two

Suppressing a shiver, Kira Marchi maneuvered her way past the throng of gamblers to the bar servicing the poker room. Management kept the casino at a temperature between morgue and meat locker, and her skimpy uniform didn't provide any warmth. The tray of empty glasses she carried shook, but at least she'd refrained from throwing an empty beer bottle at the vile man's fleshy face. The psychedelic carpet, designed to distract the patrons from the security cameras lining the ceiling, muffled the sound of her heels. She couldn't even express her frustration with a noisy stomp.

With the hot, scruffy guy who defended her honor gone, his sleazy tablemate had gotten handsy. Why did he need to grope her? He'd degraded her enough with his insults and attempts to coerce her to crawl on the carpet for a crappy tip. She wished she could conjure a force field to keep his clammy hands off her.

The shift manager claimed he hadn't seen the man grab her ass. She suspected the casino cared more about keeping a customer than an employee. In a sluggish economy, servers were the equivalent of commemorative quarters, well collected but common. Hardcore gamblers with deep pockets were the 1804 silver dollar—priceless.

To add to the shittiness of her day, her ex-boyfriend, Eddie, worked the bar. His brief stint on a reality-television dating show allowed him to claim D-list celebrity status, and he fostered the delusion that at any moment he could be swarmed by paparazzi. He focused his megawatt grin on her, and charisma oozed from his pores. His sunshine smile could melt panties and entice the droopiest plant to stand at attention. Even plastic foliage seemed to perk up in his presence. But the smile lacked the sincerity of true warmth, being as fake as his shiny veneers and spray tan.

Kira recited the list of drink orders, hoping for once he'd do his damned job and not get personal. He always wanted what he couldn't have. When she'd broken up with him, he'd pursued her harder than ever. She suspected he wanted to get back together more to soothe his bruised ego than because he genuinely cared for her.

"What can I do to convince you to come over tonight?" he asked for the eleventh time and patted his gel-stiff blond-highlighted hair. "The producers sent over a gag-reel DVD from Sin City Singles. There's a full minute of scenes featuring *moi*."

"I told you, I'm busy." Kira would rather watch static on the television than Eddie turning his charm on a bevy of bachelorettes. She didn't want to date a man who used more hair product in a week than she used in a year. Especially one who called her frigid and seemed to be on the constant lookout for a girlfriend upgrade.

"Why the rush? You got a date or something?" He placed his elbows on the bar, perfectly groomed eyebrows raised.

An image of the hot poker player came to mind. With his soulful brown eyes and dark hair, he bore a slight resemblance to one of her favorite musicians, Gavin Rossdale. The player seemed more in need of a good meal and a shave than a girlfriend, though. She shook thoughts of him from her mind. After the debacle with Eddie, she vowed never to date anyone she met at work.

"Actually, I do." And that wasn't a lie. One of the other waitresses swore the 1Night Stand dating service had changed her life. Based on the recommendation, Kira had decided to take a chance. She'd entered her personal information into the electronic form on the dating service's website the week before. It terrified her, but she couldn't pass up an opportunity to gain some experience, an impartial second opinion on her sexual performance. Hopefully, no one would call her frigid again.

As if on cue, the phone tucked in a hidden pocket of her skirt vibrated.

Eddie huffed and went off to fill the drink order.

She checked her phone. Madame Eve didn't waste time. She'd scheduled Kira's date for that night.

***

Ian pushed the plastic key into the door-lock mechanism. With a metallic buzz, the lock released and he entered. Madame Evangeline's return email had stated the voucher covered the room and all related amenities. Inside the lavish suite—decorated in an elegant palette of blacks, whites, and silvers—he gravitated toward a tray of bread, cheese, and fruit. He shoveled food in his mouth, passing over a bottle of champagne chilling in an ice bucket in favor of a Sin City amber beer from the minibar. Popping the top, he lifted the bottle in a silent toast to Madame Evangeline and took a long pull. The malts and hops in the foamy liquid lit up his taste buds and lifted his spirits. The room, a far cry from the seedy motels he'd become accustomed to, smelled faintly of flowery perfume with underlying citrus notes. The scent reminded him of one of his favorite India pale ales, a side effect of his dedication to his beloved alcoholic beverage and his former business.

A basket by the bed held a variety of lubricants

and condoms, with every color and flavor represented. Madame Evangeline had stocked the room with everything they could possibly need. Downing the beer, he opened another. Not quite the steak dinner he'd craved, but he couldn't complain.

Taking the bottle into the bathroom, Ian stripped out of his clothes. He avoided the mirror. His reflection would reveal him undeserving of this unearned luxury. What he should do was slink to the car and leave the room pristine for his date, but he'd already eaten the food, drunk the beer, and tainted the air with his bad luck, rendering the room a lost cause. And his shower would be a kindness to anyone forced to be in his close proximity. If he went another day without bathing, no amount of deodorant body spray would conceal his stench.

The shower cleared his mind and relaxed his aching muscles. He treasured so many things he'd taken for granted in his old life, such as showers and sandwiches. Some of his worries washed away, but a nagging sense of wrongness over considering ditching his date remained. But the voucher bought him the chance to get his head out of his ass and back in the game—or one last attempt to run away from his mistakes in Portland and toward a fresh start.

He hoped his date would linger in the casino and hit a slot machine jackpot. Even if she didn't hit the MegaMillions, she'd be better off without him, a MegaDud. He pictured the voucher with its elegant script print. Madame Evangeline would compensate her and provide her with a new-and-improved date.

***

Stopping at her apartment in Henderson took extra time, but Kira refused to show up for the date in her work uniform. Role-playing could be fun, but she didn't want to be reminded of her job during sex.

The Friday night traffic on the Strip crawled. Drivers and pedestrians gaped at the breathtaking Bellagio water show and the contrasting human spectacles. Kira tapped her fingers on the steering wheel and willed the light to change. The DJ on the radio stopped talking and cued up Bush's song, "Machinehead." With Gavin Rossdale belting out the lyrics, her thoughts returned to the hot poker player who'd defended her earlier. She indulged in a moment of fantasy for the duration of the song and imagined Gavin, or rather his poker-playing doppelganger, as her date.

Finally, she drove into the casino parking garage with the melody of the song still playing in her mind. Slotting her car into the first available space, she grabbed her bag and jogged into the entrance. Eddie sometimes picked up extra shifts, so she chose a path through the sea of old-school slot machines to safely avoid the poker room.

Checking the time on her cell, she elbow-bumped an elderly lady working a one-armed bandit. Her plastic bucket flipped, spilling silver coins that clinked and glinted on the patterned carpet. Perched on the edge of a wheelchair seat, she glared and muttered in a foreign language. Her companion, who appeared to be a year or so under the legal gambling age, dropped to all fours to collect the coins.

"I'm so sorry." Kira moved to help him. She stepped around the wheelchair, her foot crunching down on something hard. The object cracked in two, the sound audible even over the noisy slots.

A broken wishbone with feathers and rust-colored powder lay scattered on the carpet. The crone choked and hissed another string of guttural words, and her frantic hand gestures reminded Kira of a conductor leading an orchestra. Joining the boy on the ground, Kira helped him scoop the money and deposit it into the bucket.

"She cursed you," he said and pushed strands of his long brown hair from his gentle doe eyes.

"Excuse me?" The remaining coins she held slipped from her fingers.

"Baba said that you'll die as the moon waxes." He shrugged. "It's payback for destroying her good luck charm."

Kira eyed the broken wishbone. She'd seen some strange things since arriving in Vegas five years earlier. Until now, the trolls the bingo players favored were the scariest thing she'd encountered—the freaky, naked dolls with their rainbow hair and dead eyes unnerved her. Every gambler had a charm or a ritual to guarantee luck, but people didn't unleash death curses in the fantasy world of Sin City.

"You'd better go." He rose, replaced the bucket on

the crone's lap, and disengaged the wheelchair brake. "Baba's in a fierce mood."

The old lady kept muttering and spitting words out, her bony fingers continuing to slice the air while her hawk eyes bore into Kira's soul. As they wheeled away, Kira clutched at the nearest slot machine for balance and watched a crowd of drunken tourists swallow up the odd pair. Pins and needles traveled down her spine, and her heart banged against her breast bone. She sucked in a ragged breath and closed her eyes, and her imagination sped into overdrive. The image of the word, *curse*, scrawled on a wall in blood, formed in her mind. Her eyes popped open, and the room seemed to tilt.

No. No. No.

She couldn't let some crazy old bat and a kid freak her out. Walking through the casino to the hotel front desk with measured steps, Kira tried to make sense of the encounter. She collected the room key, took the elevator to the seventeenth floor, and tried to focus. When the doors opened, panic gripped her anew. Curses weren't real. The whole episode had to be some elaborate scam.

Sooner or later, someone would show up and offer to remove the fake curse for a large sum of money. But after living in Vegas and witnessing all sorts of scams, she'd fine-tuned her bullshit detector. She always knew when the poker players bluffed. Eddie swore her skills could land her a lucrative job in the interrogation section of the CIA. The doe-eyed boy and the crazy old lady believed in the curse. And according to Kira's roommate, beliefs powered magic. That belief or intent comprised the core of any spell. From the raw malice in the old lady's gaze, Kira had no doubt the crone wanted her dead and, if the curse failed to do the trick, she might find a more mundane instrument to get the job done.

Why the hell did this have to happen tonight? Resolving to stick with the original plan and attempt to do all the things she had been too nervous to try with Eddie, she pulled out the crumpled list she'd brainstormed while working her way through a bottle of pinot noir one night. *Sexual Bucket List* topped the page. The title, written on a lark, took on a sinister overtone as though the words had been penned by the Grim Reaper himself.

Sucking in breath after breath, Kira held each one for the count of five before letting it out. What were her options if she bailed on the date? Call Eddie and cry on his shoulder? She'd rather take her chances trying to exorcise her own demons than climb aboard that exhausting relationship treadmill again.

Straightening her clothing and smoothing her hair, she marched down the corridor. She refused to let her night be ruined. The other waitresses joked about the tourists who paid to leap off the 108th floor of the Stratosphere hotel in a controlled descent to the ground, only to lose their nerve at the top. The SkyJump gift shop sold chicken T-shirts. Kira resolved never to qualify to wear such a shirt. She'd take the plunge. For this one night, she'd put everything aside to muster the courage to go through with the date.

She rapped on the door of room 17-153. When no one answered, she knocked harder. A grizzly bear of a man in a bathrobe, carrying an ice bucket, stepped out of the room across the hall and looked her up and down. His possessive gaze had the same ick factor as the nasty man who'd fondled her in the poker room.

Fumbling with the key, she unlocked the door. Although a hotel casino employee for two years, she'd never seen the inside of one of the rooms. It struck her as odd the suite had a half-bathroom off the sitting room. The apartment she shared with her roommate didn't appear much bigger than this, and it only featured a single bath.

She looked from the ravaged room service tray to the empty beer bottle next to it. Someone's leftovers. *How romantic.* Instead of a kinky fairytale princess, she'd been cast as one of the bears who came home to the remnants of Goldilocks' bender.

She froze mid-step when a well-muscled man strode into the room, a towel wrapped around his waist. Washboard abs were an unexpected bonus. Using a second towel to dry his hair, he headed for the tray and crammed a handful of food in his mouth. A crumb clung to his facial hair. As though finally sensing her, he snapped his head up and the brown eyes of the sexy poker player met hers. *Holy crap!* She'd never expected to see him again.

Kira had been drawn to him in the poker room, but she'd wanted to be set up with a stranger, not someone to whom she'd served a beverage. While she wanted to add licking the drops of water clinging to his muscular chest to her bucket list, no good would come of hooking up with someone from the casino— even though she wanted nothing more than to experience every act on the list at least twice with him.

Her fingernails dug into the faux leather of her handbag. Now she understood the purpose of the second bathroom. A perfect refuge to hole up in and wait for checkout time, or until she decided whether to jump on him or flee.

"Did Madame Evangeline send you?" His eyes narrowed, and he tilted his head, the same expression he'd worn when evaluating the cards to determine his next move.

Oh, crap. How can he be my date?

An image of the crone's face popped into her mind. Kira's pep talk from out in the hall resurrected itself. If for only tonight, a strict *carpe diem* mentality needed to be adopted. She could either choose to believe in curses and earn the chicken shirt, or spend the night with a sexy man and get busy crossing items off her list. Dropping her purse on the floor, she moved toward him and stopped an inch away. His warm breath ruffled her hair. She imagined sucking in courage along with oxygen.

"My name is Kira Marchi. I'm your one-night stand."

Chapter Three

"Shit, I ruined this already didn't I?" Kira's gaze crawled downward toward the towel knotted around the man's slim hips before returning to lock on his eyes. "We shouldn't exchange names when this is only a one-night thing, right? Would you mind pretending I didn't introduce myself?"

His right eye twitched, and he stepped away from her. "If that's what you want. But I'd like to get to know you better." Now he looked like he wanted to hide in the half bath.

Unable to retract her words, she tried another approach. "How about a game?"

"What do you have in mind?" His right eyebrow arched.

She retrieved her purse and rooted around until she found some dice. "Whoever rolls an even number gets to ask the other person a question they have to answer. You can go first." When she passed him the dice, their fingers touched. She liked the way they felt—rough, but warm.

"What happens if you roll an odd number?" The dice danced in his palm.

She had him. "You lose your turn."

They sat on the couch with their thighs almost touching. He shook the dice, rolling an eleven on the coffee table.

"I guess I should stick to poker." His easy grin reappeared.

She threw a twelve. "What made you decide to try the dating service?"

"My luck ran cold until I emailed Madam Evangeline, but I wasn't sure about going through with the date until I looked up and saw you." Leaning toward her, he tucked a strand of hair behind her ear.

"Good answer." Her hands trembled as she scooped up the dice and rolled a hard eight. "If we could start over, what would you do?"

"Kiss you."

Kira didn't know who moved first to close the minuscule gap between them and initiate the kiss. One thing for certain, she'd never been kissed like that before—with such urgency. With such passion. Such desperation.

A caravan of tingles traveled down her body and danced in her center. But when their tongues met, the poker player applied the brakes and pulled away.

What the hell?

Resolution replaced the hunger in his expression. A hunger that had nothing to do with food and had everything to do with the promise of carnal pleasure. The kind of pleasure she'd read about in spicy romance novels and had, until now, thought to be fiction.

"We should slow down." He fussed with his towel before taking her hand and leading her to the minibar. "Would you like something to drink?"

Leaning her arm on his shoulder, Kira peered into the refrigerator. She longed to chug the dozen or so tiny bottles of spirits, but she hadn't come there to get drunk. She'd come to get laid.

"I'm good for now." *Liar.* She wouldn't be good until they were horizontal. If something didn't happen between them soon, she might lose her nerve. She couldn't return to her apartment with only her fears for company. Panic bubbled. Before it could overtake her, she grabbed at his towel.

"Hey." He loosened her grip on the fabric. "We have all night."

He'd rejected her advance. Didn't he find her attractive? *Oh hell.* What if he thought her an escort or an employee of the hotel? She tilted her head away so he couldn't see the hot flush creeping up her neck and face.

After rummaging around in the refrigerator, he extracted a beverage and passed it to her. Instead of unscrewing the cap and taking a drink, she sat on the edge of the bed and lifted the bottle to her face to cool her cheeks then picked at the label until it separated from the plastic. Sitting next to her, he removed the naked bottle from her grip, leaving her clutching the soggy paper. *Crap.*

"You're shaking." He placed his arm around her and pulled her close.

Breathing in his clean, soapy scent, she mentally ran through her sexual bucket list. Six feet or so of hot male fresh from the shower would go perfectly with item number three, a blow job. But did she dare grab the towel again? Could this time be the charm? If not, she'd leave and beg Madame Eve for another date.

Kira ran a palm along the sinewy contours of his back and neck and massaged the taut muscles. A sigh released from deep in his chest. Taking that as a sign of surrender, she buried her hand in his thick, dark hair. He ran his fingers along her jawline and up to her cheekbones. Her heart fluttered in her chest. She dared not breathe.

"What do you want?" he asked.

Her mind spun. Where should she start? Would it be weird if she consulted the wish list or blurted out she wanted to suck his dick? Rattling off all the items on the list didn't seem right either. Then she knew.

"You."

His hands cradled her face. This time, when their tongues met, there'd be no stopping. Planting kisses on her neck and collarbone, he unbuttoned her silk blouse. No man had ever turned her on like that, and they had yet to move past foreplay. Echoes of Eddie's complaints about her performance rose unbidden in her mind. Now she had some complaints for him, too. She pushed all thoughts of her ex-boyfriend from her mind.

More than ready to cross number three from her list, she arched. While her date's gaze focused on demi-bra clad breasts, she yanked off his towel.

Damn. She'd never seen a cock so large. Could she take all of him in her mouth? Resolving to find out and before he could protest, she gripped him. It jerked when her hand closed around it, hardening immediately. Emboldened, she knelt on the plush carpet and took him in her mouth. His hands tangled in her long hair. He wouldn't push her away again; he wanted this as much as she did.

Exploring his length with her tongue, she experienced the silky skin, his salty taste igniting her desire. She gripped the base, moving in time with her mouth, varying the tempo. A longing ache rose between her legs. Taking him deep in her throat, she reached down to cup his balls. The moisture in her center grew. *Who knew pleasuring a man could be such a rush?*

Releasing him, she ran her tongue over her lower lip. He beheld her with intensity, suggesting he wouldn't take his attention from her even if the hotel burned down around them. Having him nude while she stood before him clothed turned her on, but she needed to even the playing field. She rose and unfastened the last button of her blouse.

He wore the same expression he'd had when she'd walked in—as if he wanted to devour her like he had the tray of food. He stepped closer, kissing his taste from her. *Damn, can he get any sexier?*

She snaked her arms around him, holding tight, and he clung to her for a moment before pushing her against the wall. Undoing the tiny front clasp on her bra, he exposed her breasts. The air conditioning hit her bare flesh and she shivered.

The warmth of his skin traveled straight to her core. He tasted and stroked her breasts, his teeth skimming her nipples. A gasp of pleasure escaped her lips when he continued his journey, stopping to flick his tongue around her belly-button ring before unzipping her jeans.

She expected him to remove her G-string, but he seemed intent on tormenting her first. He knelt and stroked the tiny triangle of fabric. Exhaling warm breath through the lace, he hooked his finger around the string, pulling it taut. When she thought she couldn't stand it a moment longer, he worked a finger underneath the material to stroke her clit.

"You're so wet for me."

She gasped and braced against the wall to keep from oozing onto the floor, her muscles pure liquid.

His finger moved lower. When she sighed in approval, he placed one then two fingers inside her. He moved them in and out, excruciatingly slowly. With the tremors of an orgasm building, she moaned. He added a third finger, stretching her, bringing his mouth closer. His beard stubble brushed her sensitive skin and, when his tongue found her clit, she exploded.

Before she could collect herself, he shoved aside the tray of food, picked her up, and settled her on the table. Kira let out a squeak of protest when he stepped away to dig into the hospitality basket. He soon returned with a gold foil square. Tearing the packet open, he removed a condom. Thank goodness, he'd remembered protection because she'd forgotten all about the strip of condoms in her purse.

"Let me," she said, mentally ticking off number four. In high school health class, the teacher had instructed them on how to sheath a banana with a condom. Kira had longed for the opportunity to slide latex over flesh instead of fruit, but her previous lovers, in their hurry to get laid, refused to wait for her trembling fingers to work it on. Tonight she could ask for whatever she wanted.

When she fumbled with the condom, she expected him to scold her and take over, but he seemed content to watch her handle his cock. Taking her time, she arranged the reservoir tip on the head and unrolled it, inch by inch.

"My name—" he began, but she interrupted him with a finger to his lips. Anonymous sex would be better than getting attached.

Naked, except for the condom, he stood statue-still. His erection dipped, and instead of touching her, he stared at her. She wanted to scream at him for making her wait to feel him inside of her. *Does he want me to beg for it?*

He shook his head in a mental reboot and reached for her breast. Holding it in his palm, he captured the nipple in his mouth. Kira arched into him with a mewling cry. Burning for him, she scooted to the edge of the table and lifted her legs.

He rubbed the tip of his cock against her clit then eased into her, slowly at first. Each push and retreat ramped her desire, but she wanted it harder, faster. She met his strokes, and her eagerness seemed to encourage him. He let out a groan, as though she'd broken through his resolve to be gentle, and drove into her.

The tremors built again. Longing to call out the name of her lover, she hit dead ends and blanks until a name rose to the surface and escaped her lips. "Gavin!" She bucked, riding out the most intense orgasm she'd ever experienced.

He tensed, a sheen of sweat covering him. With his eyes closed tight, he gave a final thrust and let out a grunt of release. In the haze of afterglow, the inky blackness of dread settled in. She'd cried the name of the musician her poker player vaguely resembled.

Wrong name. *Very* wrong name.

Chapter Four

Ian studied the beautiful woman impaled on his cock. It all made sense now. She didn't want him to tell her his name, because she wanted to pretend he was Gavin. Whoever that was. *Lucky bastard.* But if she wanted someone else, why had she signed up for the date?

When Kira had taken him between her lips, he couldn't help but think of Dick's cruel comment about her spending time on her knees. Then, she drove all thoughts of the asshole from his mind. As much as Ian wanted to exorcise the phantom Gavin from his brain as well, Kira could call him by whatever name she wanted, if only he could make love to her again.

Her pale inner thighs showed the contact burn

from his beard stubble. *I should have requested a razor from the front desk.* Before he pulled out, he placed a kiss on her soft cheek. Removing the condom, he wrapped it in a napkin and dropped it into the wastebasket.

What should he talk about with someone who didn't want to know his name? Not that they had to talk. He had plenty of thoughts on how to spend the rest of their time together. No words were necessary for any of them.

She stood in front of the window with its view of the Strip.

"How about some champagne?" He'd happily switch from beer to wine for her.

Turning toward him, she nodded, wide-eyed, and crossed her arms over voluminous breasts.

He recognized the fear in her eyes. She didn't do casual sex or one-night stands, arranged by a high-end dating service or not. Ian wanted to make her comfortable so she'd stay the rest of the night. If she walked out now, he'd never have the opportunity to really know her and for her to want to know him. To beg him not only for his name, but for the dark secret that ripped apart his insides and stole his sleep. And to convince him of his worthiness for her love. At best, he could hope she'd acknowledge him if they crossed paths in the casino.

"There's a bathrobe in the closet." Speaking the words pained him. If he had his way, she'd spend their entire time together nude.

"I'll go freshen up." Heading to the closet, she removed the robe and went into the bathroom. The door closed with a click.

Ian untwisted the wire from the neck of the bottle, removed the metal foil covering the cork, and tugged. The cork shot out and slammed into a lamp. With a curse, he checked for damage and found it unbroken. Letting out a sigh of relief, he straightened the shade. Property damage probably didn't count as an amenity.

Used to tapping kegs and opening beer bottles, he hadn't uncorked bubbly in years. At least Kira hadn't witnessed his ineptitude. He poured the champagne into two flutes, added a strawberry to each, and used the sink in the half bath to clean up. When he finished, he raided the tray of food again. And waited.

When she hadn't emerged after a while, he tapped on the door. "Are you okay?"

She didn't respond.

It would be unforgivable to do something to hurt or frighten her. But what if something else was wrong? She could be hurt or unconscious and unable to call for help. He tied his towel around his waist. It wouldn't do to burst in on her buck naked.

Twisting the knob, Ian pushed the door open. Clad in the bathrobe, Kira sat in the empty sunken tub, sobbing. *Shit.* He knew how to be an accountant, a dealer in numbers and data—not emotion. A coldhearted decision to value the mighty dollar over the safety of his employees had brought him to Vegas. This time he needed to meet emotion head on.

The door creaked, and Kira peeked between her fingers. The man hesitated before entering the room then crept toward her as though treading through a minefield. *Great, he probably thinks I'm a nut case.* Not only had she called him the wrong name, she'd gotten a glimpse of the waxing moon and ice-cold fear had paralyzed her. Stupid old hag and her damned curses. Sinking farther into the tub, Kira wished she could hide under soapy water.

She'd been superstitious her whole life, developing a daily ritual of consulting the horoscope for her sun sign, Gemini. Been careful never to break a mirror, open an umbrella inside the house, or walk under a ladder. Always tossed spilt salt over her left shoulder and picked pennies off the ground. The crone's curse nagged at her. It might not be real, but Kira needed to talk to her roommate, a self-proclaimed expert on all things occult.

"I'm fine," she said, and cleared her throat.

"May I join you?" His gentle tone soothed her. At her nod, he darted out of the room.

While she examined the tidy row of miniature bottles of soap, shampoo, conditioner, and bath salts, she imagined him calling the concierge for a psych-ward recommendation. *Do mental hospitals take reservations?*

He returned a moment later, clutching feather pillows in one hand and half-full flutes with the other. After retrieving the champagne bottle, he topped off the glasses and set the bottle on the floor.

Kira accepted a glass and leaned forward, allowing him to tuck a pillow between her back and the tub. Arranging the other pillow across from her, he settled against it.

"To our fortuitous second meeting." He clinked his glass with hers.

"Second meeting?"

"You brought me the voucher I left at the poker table and a bottle of water." He raised his eyebrows. "I couldn't tip you before, but I can make it up to you now."

Multiple orgasms were much better payment than mere cash. She sipped the bubbly liquid. A firm strawberry bobbed up and down in the glass, brushing her mouth, reminding her of his cock between her lips.

"Tell me what's wrong." He stroked her wrist, his thumb moving in small circles. Something tightened in her center, his touch reminiscent of his masterful manipulation of her feminine bits.

"It's nothing," she lied.

He pulled his hand away and took a big gulp of champagne. "If you want to be alone...."

"It's not that. I'd rather talk about you."

"I don't understand." He raked his fingers through his hair. "You didn't want to know my name. Am I supposed to pretend to be Gavin?"

"Huh?" Then it dawned on her. "I'm sorry I called you by someone else's name. Did anyone ever mention you look a little like Gavin Rossdale from Bush?"

His brows knit together. "Are you saying you want to have sex with a rock star?"

"Is that a trick question?" She smirked. "It's the idea of sex with someone I just met and whose name I didn't know that's exciting. A fantasy, I guess."

His eyes lit with interest. "Do you have other fantasies you want to explore?"

"Maybe." Kira pursed her lips.

"Will you share them with me?"

One thing for sure, she wouldn't make the mistake of calling him Gavin again. "I will if you'll share a couple things with me first."

"Okay, what do you want to know?" He settled deeper against the pillow and propped his arms against the edge of the tub.

"I want to know what brought you to Vegas." She shifted, relaxing one leg out over the side. "And I want to know your name."

He picked up his glass and swirled the strawberry around. "My name is Ian Harding." He drained the champagne, leaving the fruit. "I came to Vegas because I killed a man."

Chapter Five

Ian waited for Kira to order him to leave. What the hell had possessed him to blurt out this confession? His subconscious must be hell-bent on destroying his undeserved moment of pleasure. If he could unspeak the words, he would. She wouldn't want to be alone with him now, defenseless and practically naked.

Kira grabbed the champagne bottle and held it by its neck, as though she planned to swing it at him. Her need for a makeshift weapon pained him. He sighed and scooted over to give her a clear path to the door.

"I promise not to hurt you. I didn't mean to kill him. You could call it an accident, I guess."

"Tell me the whole story, or I'll leave." Her gaze on

the door, she kept a white-knuckled grip on the bottle. Like a model rocket with a lit fuse, she looked ready to launch.

"Please don't go." His words were scratchy and broken. Why hadn't he told her he'd come to Vegas to become a professional poker player? Because he couldn't lie—she deserved to know the whole story.

The event triggering his trip to Vegas gave him nightmares, and now it would destroy this brief waking dream. The words tumbled out of his mouth. "A man died because of me."

She narrowed her eyes. "Go on."

"My brother, Derek, and I own a microbrewery in Portland. We were days from making a deal with a major beer distributor, but Derek didn't want to sell. He liked the way things were." Speaking his brother's name reminded Ian of his cell phone, and the emails and texts he couldn't bear to read.

"Keep going."

"He asked me to sign off on some new equipment. At the close of the deal, the manufacturing operation would transfer to the purchaser's factory in Wisconsin so I didn't see any point to the upgrades."

Ian sighed. "One of our employees died when a tank exploded."

"Did the tank malfunction?"

"I left before the release of the results of the investigation."

"So how do you know you're responsible?" Holding her robe closed, Kira placed the bottle in the tub, climbed out, and settled on the floor next to him. As though knowing he'd been carrying knots in his neck for weeks, she worked to loosen them.

"I just know." He couldn't explain the roundhouse to the gut every time he remembered the coroner rolling out the body bag. Or the odor of charred meat that clung to his nostrils. Ian had killed the man as surely as if he'd used a handgun or a hunting knife. If only he had thought with his heart instead of his wallet. "Are you going to run screaming from the building now that you know the kind of man I am?"

Kira shifted her ministrations to his upper back. His body sang under her magic touch. "Maybe you screwed up. The important thing is to stop doing it. You'll feel better once you return to Oregon and face everything head on."

46

He placed his head in his hands. How could he go back there when he couldn't even muster the courage to listen to his brother's messages or read his texts?

She tilted his head up. "So you ran away to Vegas? Why?"

"Penance, I guess. I wanted to live without using any money I earned from the brewery."

"How's that working out for you?" The corners of her mouth twitched.

"I'm in a luxury hotel with a bewitching brunette. It doesn't get any better." Ian decided to press his luck. "Are you willing to share a fantasy now?"

"I have a list, actually," she said, and examined the ceiling tiles. "I read about the reverse cowgirl position in a magazine. I've always wanted to try it." She glanced at him and bit her lip.

Ian pictured her, facing away, riding him, and wearing only a cowboy hat. His cock tented the towel he still wore. *Oh hell yes.* He definitely wanted to fulfill that particular fantasy. If only he hadn't ruined his chance with talk of his screwed-up past.

"Good one. Let's hear another." He cleared his throat.

"Nice try, buster." She poked him with a glittery, polished nail. "I have a better idea, involving fantasy number seven. Pour us refills."

He rose to obey with cartoon sevens dancing a conga line in his mind.

She removed the pillow and bottle from the tub, opened the faucet and dumped bath salts in the water. Bubbles formed, and the aroma of roses and jasmine filled the air. After refilling their glasses, they clinked them and watched the tub fill.

Kira shut off the water and let her robe fall to the tile. With a toss of her hair, she returned his gaze. "Are you going to join me?"

He couldn't wrap his mind around the knowledge his revelation hadn't scared her off. His cock twitched at the sight of her perfect, rounded ass. All too soon, though, the bubbles hid her exquisite, naked form. Setting their glasses on the floor, he dropped his towel, and climbed in behind her.

"Tell me more about these fantasies. How many are we talking about?"

"Only seven," she said. "And we've already covered a few of them."

Lucky number seven. Only in Vegas.

Dipping a washcloth in the soapy water, he ran it along her shoulder blades. Tendrils of hair curled around her long neck. He trailed kisses down her spine. Goose bumps erupted along her skin, and she pressed against his cock. Ian wanted to explore every inch of her with his hands and mouth. Maybe he didn't deserve these stolen moments, but he couldn't deny her if she'd have him.

She reached behind her, along his thighs to his cock, and stroked his length. Letting the washcloth drop, he curved his palms around to cup her full breasts. Her nipples hardened under his touch. Still holding one breast, he ran one hand down her skin and eased a finger inside her pussy.

She jerked and shuddered. Her breath came out in gasps.

He needed to be balls deep in her. *Now.* "Ready for the rodeo, darlin'?"

"Yes," she replied, the word soft but sure.

He climbed out and scooped her up, holding her tightly against his body. The trust in her eyes undid him. He hadn't earned it, but he swore she would never regret giving it to him.

It killed him to do it, but he set her down and dried her skin with a fresh towel. They walked hand in hand to the bed, stopping so he could snag a condom from the welcome basket.

He'd be happy to make every fantasy on her list come true. With eyes alight with anticipation, she reached for the packet. Condom secured, she seemed unsure what to do next.

"Come on," he urged, joining her on the bed. Settling on his stomach, she faced away from him.

He sat up and wrapped his arms around her. "My beautiful cowgirl."

Her muscles constricted with tension. All of her bravado must have gone down the drain with the bath water. Gripping her hair, he pushed her forward enough for her pussy to reach his groin. Within moments, she relaxed, primed and ready. She scooted into position and settled over him with care. His cock sank, inch by inch, into her tight heat. Damn, she felt like home. Ian fought the urge to control the rhythm. The position had made Kira's oh-too-short fantasy list, and she had to be the one to call the shots.

The scent from the bath salts mixed with the musky scent of sex, surrounding them in a decadent cocoon. Her movements started out jerky and unsure, but smoothed out as she experimented with different rhythms. Not that he cared. He could watch her bounce on his cock all day. Once she seemed more confident, he thrust to meet her. He'd make certain she earned her cowgirl badge.

She peered over her shoulder, her eyes hooded. Her cheeks were pink and her wet hair tousled.

"Any other requests, darlin?" he asked with an extra twang. Not an outdoorsman, he'd never appreciated the fun of cowgirl games. Until now.

"More," she panted.

A request he'd be happy to fulfill. He could become addicted to this woman. Lifting her off him, he eased her onto the comforter and slipped his cock inside then held her wrists and pinned them over her head with one hand.

"Oh, yeah," she cried.

He pounded into her and, with each stroke, she gave a moan of satisfaction. He shifted to get better leverage to go even deeper and she clawed the sheets, writhing, convulsing around his cock, shouting his name before finally falling limp beneath him.

She'd called his name. *My name.*

He thrust again, and his orgasm hit. With his pulse thrumming, heart pounding, and hope returning, he savored every second spent inside her.

Easing out, Ian dropped beside her and held her close. Their breathing slowed, hearts beating in unison. If he never had to leave the room, he'd be a happy man. But with that thought came another—how could he let her go when their time together ended?

Chapter Six

Ian dozed but kept waking up after short bursts of sleep. He needed to see Kira cuddled next to him to convince himself she hadn't been a perfect dream. Each time he awoke, he breathed in her sweet scent, thankful for his good fortune in winning the date and the chance to win Kira's heart. With her by his side, he might be able to summon the courage to face his brother. And the life he'd left behind in Portland.

What were the odds his date would be the beautiful cocktail waitress who'd returned the voucher? He didn't believe in coincidences. *Did Madame Evangeline know Kira would be the one to convince me to face my past?*

He had never imagined transitioning from

successful businessman to down-on-his-luck gambler in a week. Maybe he had a little luck left in him. For all of his sins, though, he didn't deserve such a blessing. But, deserve it or not, he had no intention of denying this woman anything she wished.

Facing him, she ground against his morning wood, a wicked, ready-for-another-fantasy grin plastered on her face.

"Mornin', beautiful." He stroked her hair.

"Good morning, Ian." She stretched and the blanket shifted, exposing her collarbone, oh-so-kissable throat, and pert, naked breasts.

His cock responded to the sound of his name. Before they made love, he needed assurance that the end of the date didn't mean the end of their relationship. He'd never been lucky at love before, but he was well acquainted with the fickleness of fortune.

Playing with a lock of hair curling around her breast, he said, "Let's go to Red Rock Canyon this weekend. I hear it's a great place to view the full moon."

She stiffened, and the smile melted.

Not the response he'd expected. They hadn't even had breakfast, and he couldn't resist a desperate plea to see her again. He laced their fingers together and changed the subject. "Want something to eat? I'll call for room service. We can get a full spread—waffles, bacon, eggs, and juice." His stomach growled.

She wrenched away from him, her face frozen in an unreadable mask. Moving to the edge of the king-sized bed, she yanked the coverlet over her sexy curves.

With her ferocious appetite for sex, he hadn't taken her for someone who hated breakfast. "Just coffee then? Or tea? Maybe they can send up one of those plastic bears filled with honey. I can drizzle it on you and have you for breakfast."

She shook her head, her face turning the greenish yellow of a fading bruise.

Well, shit. Everything he'd told her about his responsibility in the death of his employee and his subsequent flight from his old life must have finally sunk in. What woman would want to stay with a coward who couldn't face his problems? A broke gambler with a shady past, he couldn't offer her much in terms of a future. She must see a hundred people a day who believed gambling would solve all of their problems. But he'd bet on her no matter what the odds.

A sharp rap on the door caused her to jerk and roll off the bed. She popped up and tightened the blanket around her body. As close as they had been, seeing her act skittish caused an emptiness in the pit of his stomach, and it had nothing to do with his desire for breakfast.

"Housekeeping," someone called from the other side of the door.

Ian didn't bother to hide his annoyance over the interruption. "Can you come back later?"

"Yes, sorry," came the reply.

Kira crept away from him. When he climbed off the bed to go to her, she held up a hand to stop him. Gathering her clothing they'd strewn the night before, she retreated to the bathroom. He racked his brain trying to think of something to convince her to stay. Unable to promise her a future, he had nothing to offer except sex.

A few minutes later, she shuffled into the

bedroom, her shirt hanging askew on the right side, the buttons improperly matched with the holes. Ian crossed his arms to keep from embracing her. She couldn't leave like this. He'd do anything to convince her to stay. Head lowered, Kira walked toward him, and his heart whirled in his chest like the reels on a slot machine. But no matter the thrill of watching cherries and sevens and jackpot symbols spin by, all jaded gamblers knew the odds favored a losing draw.

"You're a good man. I can't tell you how much this meant to me." She touched his face.

Undoing her shirt, he kissed each breast before fastening the buttons properly.

"Life is too short to run from your problems. You never really escape them, you know?"

Before he could respond, she stood on tiptoes and pressed her lips to his.

He put everything he couldn't say into the kiss and twined his fingers in her hair. She matched his passion before pushing him away. Dragging her purse by its long strap, she headed out the door.

The divining rod of his erection pointed toward the closed door. Toward the woman who'd become his whole world in one night. Toward the woman he couldn't let leave.

Yanking on his boxer shorts, he bolted after her. The elevator door slid shut as the suite door slammed behind him. *Shit.* He'd left the stupid key on the table by the bed. If only he hadn't wasted time with his underwear. He padded up to the maid in his bare feet. Her eyes like saucers, she wedged her cart between them. She kept one hand on the handle and wielded a toilet brush with the other, evidently ready to run him over or swat him. She must think him a pervert. He might as well have been naked.

"If you let me into my room, I promise to check out within ten minutes."

Keeping the brush pointed at him, she used her master key to open the door for him to enter. He couldn't breathe with Kira gone. She had taken all of the oxygen with her.

He threw on his clothes and, on impulse collected the remainder of the tiny containers of bath salts. Unscrewing the top off one, Ian inhaled the scent that would forever remind him of their bath.

He vowed to get his business in order and prove

himself to be the kind of man she deserved.

Chapter Seven

The bells and clicks of slot machine wheels spinning greeted Ian on his way through McCarran International Airport. He hauled his carry-on items, a bulky parcel, and a leather duffle bag, to the taxi waiting area, skipping baggage claim. Three days earlier, he'd completed the sixteen-hour drive to his home in Portland and fallen into a deep, dreamless sleep. When he awoke, he'd showered, dressed, and set about facing his past.

Pushing through the remorse and fear, he'd met with his brother, as well as their lawyer and the wife of the employee who had died. With papers signed and bridges not quite mended but definitely in a state of repair, he booked a flight to Las Vegas. After demolishing the barriers from his past, he wanted to build the foundation for his future.

Ian slid into the backseat of a silver sequin-covered taxi advertising the newest Cirque du Soleil show and told the driver to take him to the casino where Kira worked. Each of the landmarks of the Strip they passed—the Luxor pyramid, the giant gold MGM lion, and the Eiffel Tower—brought him closer to her. He wanted to cheer when the driver steered the Prius onto the winding driveway of the casino.

Ian handed him money, waved off his change, and headed into the casino entrance. This time he didn't do a walk of shame across the colorful carpet, instead held his head high, a man at peace with his past and hopeful about his future.

He scanned the poker room and the adjacent bar, but he didn't see any sign of Kira. The bartender, a boy-band member wannabe with a plastic smile and shellacked blond hair, sang when Ian slipped him a hundred dollar bill for information. Kira would be working the evening shift.

Needing a distraction to stop his mad chronicling of the slow journey of the second hand on his watch, Ian settled into a seat at a poker table. Of course, the idiot from the other night played at the only no-limit Texas Hold 'Em game running. Ian kept an eye on the casino floor for Kira, barely paying attention to the game.

Two hours later, after a string of straights, flushes, and full houses, the mound of chips Ian had accumulated astounded him.

"Do you think you're Doyle Brunson or something, playing without looking at your hand?" Dick flicked cigar ash in Ian's direction. "I raise."

If the guy wanted to compare him to a poker legend, Ian would take it as a compliment. He pretended to peek at his cards, but he couldn't focus on them with Kira due to arrive. His brain registered a pair of red twos. A small pocket pair didn't have a great chance of winning. He should fold, but his adversary had finally spoken to him. He couldn't help but play out the hand, so he called. From the prior radio silence, he'd assumed the bastard hadn't recognized him clean-shaven and wearing a Brooks Brothers suit and tie.

The dealer dealt out the flop, the ten of diamonds, two of clubs, and three of spades.

Ian had a set, three of a kind. Lady Luck came through yet again.

Dick squinted at him, rotated the cigar in his mouth, and pushed a stack of chips forward.

The dealer counted the chips. "Three hundred to call."

Ian matched the bet.

The other players folded as though their cards were coated with poison rather than plastic. An odd sense of *déjà vu* overtook him. Except for Kira's presence, all the elements seemed to match up with the last time he'd played one-on-one with Dick. If she showed up and the asshole dared to insult her, he'd deck the son of a bitch and let the chips fall where they may. Literally.

"Two players." The dealer removed the casino's cut and dealt the turn, the seven of hearts.

With the rainbow of suits on the board, Ian could rule out a flush.

Dick bet another three hundred dollars.

Ian considered raising, but not wanting to scare off his opponent, only called the bet.

The dealer placed the river on the table—the

queen of hearts. Kira held the title of the queen of his heart. The other player pushed all of his chips forward.

Ian examined the board. No straight possibilities. With the early raise, his opponent likely had a pair of tens with an ace kicker. Loving his aces, the jerk always raised when he had an ace in the hole. Ian's set of deuces might be the best hand. The queen of hearts seemed to wink at him.

"I call." He pushed the remainder of his stack forward.

Dick displayed his tobacco-stained, shark-tooth grin and revealed his pocket aces.

"I've got a set," Ian announced flipping over his hand. Then, he gaped at the two of diamonds and three of hearts on the table in front of him. Shit, he didn't have a pair of twos to make three of a kind with the two of clubs on the board like he'd thought. He only had a two and a three. His face heated with the realization that again he'd let the other man get the better of him.

"Two pair, deuces and treys." The dealer nudged the two of clubs and the three of spades on the board.

Ian sank his fingers into the mountain of chips the dealer pushed toward him. "Oh, I forgot about the three of spades on the board." He couldn't contain his grin. *All hail Lady Luck.*

"Floor, I need the floor." Dick waved frantically at the poker room manager, a tall woman with metal eyeglasses and silver hair in a bun. "This shyster," the sore loser pointed at Ian, venom lacing his words, "said he had a set of deuces, but he only had two pair."

"Okay." The manager surveyed everything on the table. "So, this gentleman said he had a hand that beat you, when actually he had a different hand that beat you. Is that correct?"

Ian rubbed his neck. "I should have taken a better look."

"Mr. Richards, I'm sorry to inform you, but the only way you could have won is if your opponent had folded. It doesn't matter what he verbalized. The cards stand."

The irate man slammed his fist down on the table. "Bring me a rack of black on my marker."

Ian caught sight of Kira then, wearing jeans and a

fitted black T-shirt. She headed toward the bar. Reaching under the table, he extracted three plastic racks, and stacked his chips into them.

"You can't leave," Dick bellowed. "You have to give me the chance to win back my money."

Ian could have schooled the bastard on respect, but his opponent failed to rouse his ire. He had nothing but pity for the mean-spirited man, the type who had a miserable life and needed to denigrate others to bring them into the gutter with him. Done screwing around, Ian stood, bounty in hand.

A petite cocktail waitress with Marilyn Monroe blonde hair and bright-red lipstick sidled up to the table. "Drinks?"

Ian extracted two stacks of chips from the tray, passing one to the dealer and one to the cocktail waitress. She deserved an extra-big tip for having to serve the jerk who would never develop manners and learn to treat people with respect. "Have a great night." Picking up his parcel and duffle bag, he headed to the poker room cashier. The manager reached for Ian's racks to cash him out.

"One thousand, seven hundred and fifty dollars,"

she said counting out the chips and exchanging them for crisp bills.

Ian passed the fifty to her before shoving the wad of bills into his pocket.

"Thank you, sir. We hope to see you again soon." She caressed the bill lovingly before dropping the money into a clear Lucite box labeled *tips*.

"Don't count on it," he muttered. He might play poker again for fun, but it would never be a career. He had a new-and-improved strategy for the future.

He exited the poker room with the idea of having Dick's money weighing on him. Extracting the cash, he returned his buy-in money of two hundred dollars to his pocket. He searched the casino seeking a worthy recipient for his fifteen hundred dollars in winnings. A constipated-looking elderly woman in a wheelchair scowled at the Triple Seven slot machine in front of her. Dropping in three coins, she pulled the handle. It had to be a sign. Kira had seven items on her fantasy list, making the number magic for him. But Ian planned to expand her list to seventy. Or seven thousand.

The money burned hot in his hand.

"Good evening, ma'am."

Eyes narrowed into slits, the woman muttered under her breath, her foreign words and rough tone grating the air like sandpaper.

Holy crap, she's pegged me a thief, ready to steal her bucket of coins or her lucky machine.

Actions spoke louder than words. Ian extended the currency. A liver-spotted hand shot out, and the money disappeared. He'd never dreamed she could move so fast. Her face transformed into the caricature of a jack-o-lantern's snaggle-toothed grin.

The hair on his nape stood up, and he dropped the items he held. The urge to throw salt over his shoulder overwhelmed him. She spooked him.

"Okay, then," he said, backing away.

The old woman grabbed his arm, her skin colder than a slab of beef straight from the freezer. He wanted to pull away, but he imagined her brittle bones snapping off with the claw-like hand still attached to his limb.

"You're welcome." He blinked the image of her handless arm from his mind and carefully pried open her fingers. "Have a nice evening," he added, scanning the casino for Kira.

He let out his breath when he confirmed she was engaged in an animated conversation with the bartender. Ian glanced at his watch. Her shift should have started by now. Scooping up his belongings, he headed across the expanse of the casino toward his future.

Chapter Eight

"You're wasting my time." Kira should have left the resignation letter in her supervisor's mailbox and foregone trying to explain her decision to quit to Eddie. Even though he'd gotten her the transfer to the poker room, she didn't owe him anything anymore. Not even an explanation for her decision.

"There's a waiting list for cocktail waitress positions. If you reapply later, your name goes to the bottom of the queue." He ignored the customer waving for his attention at the other end of the bar.

"I'm not going to reapply." Like most conversations with Eddie, this one moved in an endless loop of nothing.

"Look, I'm sorry if I made working here

uncomfortable for you."

This was no time for a heart-to-heart. After spending three nights plagued with nightmares featuring the old woman, and with the full moon only a day away, Kira had decided to visit a voodoo priestess in New Orleans known for removing curses. If the curse could be lifted, she'd look for a job at the casinos near the French Quarter. Her luck had run out in Vegas, and whether she was destined for a tragic end or fresh start, she needed to be somewhere other than Sin City. "My resignation has nothing to do with you."

"What if we got back together? Would you stay then?" Eddie spoke the words fast, as though he knew once she walked away, he would never see her again.

She pointed toward the gesturing customer. "You'd better get that guy's drink before he gets pissed and leaves."

But Eddie no longer focused on her. He stared behind her, mouth open and eyebrows scrunched together. Kira recognized the look. She'd lost him. Whatever intense desperation he had mustered up had flittered away at the sight of some hot chick he wanted to bed.

She needed to get to the airport. To make up time, she'd leave her resignation letter with him. She removed the legal-sized envelope from her shoulder bag and placed it on the bar. "Give this to Mr. Otto."

"Do you know that guy?" He nodded to indicate someone behind her.

Kira spun, annoyed at Eddie's stalling tactics. Her breath caught when she glimpsed Ian striding toward her carrying a duffle bag and a large box. She grabbed a barstool for support. The final stage of the crone's curse must be some cruel, full-on hallucination. But Ian had a new confident air about him. And he wore a charcoal suit and a tie.

"Hey, Kira," he said.

Goose bumps crawled down her arms at the sound of his deep voice. She went limp when he hugged her. Burying her head against his chest, she breathed in the scent of his woodsy cologne. Her nipples stiffened as she remembered his hands exploring her skin. Tears welled, and she let out an involuntary sniffle.

"I took your advice and talked to my brother about the accident and the business."

"And?" She met his gaze again. "What happened?"

"The toxicology results confirmed the man who died had high levels of narcotics in his bloodstream. His personnel records showed a history of addiction. One more strike, and he'd have been fired. Another employee reported the man had been behaving erratically before the accident."

"I'm so happy everything is working out for you." She hugged him hard, and the box he held clattered to the ground.

"Not only for me. For us. I'm going to use my share of the business to open a microbrewery in Vegas." He held her face in his palms. "I want to make a future here with you."

If only such a thing were possible. "You came back for me?" Her words were soft and low, like a prayer.

"Hell yeah." He reached for the box. "I have something for you. Shut your eyes."

Hating the idea of closing her eyes and missing out on seeing him, she complied. She wanted to spend every one of her final moments looking at her sexy hunk but couldn't deny him anything he asked.

She heard the sound of tissue paper rustling.

When she thought she couldn't stand it anymore, the smell of leather filled her nose, and a weight settled on her head.

Opening one eye, she peeked at him.

"Here." He turned her to face the mirror behind the bar. "A present for my sexy cowgirl."

Kira examined her reflection and the Stetson hat she wore. Her cheeks warmed with the memory of riding him.

She kissed him, expressing her feelings with her mouth and tongue. His erection ground against her leg. If he wanted to take her right there, she doubted she'd stop him.

Epilogue

Esmeralda clutched the cash to her bosom, rattling the bucket of silver coins on her lap. Once she returned home, she would add the money to the small sum she had saved for her grandson's escape from his arranged marriage. Cam needed to travel across the country to avoid his father's influence and power. Having arranged her daughter's marriage to Cam's father, she could only blame herself for her grandson's predicament.

The handsome man who'd given her the money moved through the casino, coming to a halt behind a dark-haired woman. Esmerelda decided to cast a spell of protection on the man to reward him for his kindness. Her beliefs required no less. If she failed to do so, bad juju would cling to the money and bring misfortune when spent.

"Follow him," she ordered Cam, digging into the cavernous purse pinned between her boney knees and the bucket containing her gambling money. Complying, her grandson pushed the wheelchair toward the bar.

Esmeralda's nose twitched when she registered the faint, rancid odor of an executed curse. She recognized the signature of her spell work. Her benefactor was speaking to the devil woman who'd destroyed her grandson's charm.

"Grandma," Cam asked. "You can break your curse, right?"

He spoke as though tossing out a dare. *Stupid boy.* He fancied himself a romantic, holding out for true love. Without her help, he would be forever trapped in a loveless marriage to his cousin. Her worthless daughter had made the deal while pregnant with the boy.

Esmerelda spat on the ground. If Cam only knew she'd made the charm, the one the woman had broken, for him. The materials had been expensive and difficult to obtain, and she hadn't enough left to construct a second charm. She had unleashed the curse to ensure the woman would pay for ruining her grandson's chance to find true love.

She should show him the folly of love. The only things that mattered were family, fortune, and eye-for-an-eye justice. The devil woman should get what she deserved for destroying the charm. Once Esmeralda cast a forgetfulness spell on the man, he would find someone else to love. Maybe a woman in this very casino.

"Please, Grandma. Give them a happy ending." Cam's hazel eyes seemed to plead along with his words.

She took another look. The couple kissed. The man cupped the woman's face with his hands, and she had one hand around the man's back and another firmly clasped around his ass.

Slut.

The memory of an illicit night in the woods with her true love before her own arranged marriage struck Esmerelda. The painful bumps of stinging nettle had covered her backside but done nothing to wipe the satisfied grin from her face. That man had some magic of his own. Their one special night of passion helped her accept a long, loveless marriage.

She made her decision. "Curse," she said, pulling a bag of herbs from the folds of her skirt.

Cam's face fell.

"You have the gift, boy. Use it now to see how I bend the curse," she said in her native language. While chanting the words of the spell, she studied her grandson. She lit the herbs in an ashtray and waved her hand to disperse the smoke.

Her nemesis made a choking noise, followed by a hacking cough. From their distance, Cam couldn't see the death mark uncurl from the woman's flesh, but Esmeralda expected him to sense the change.

His eyes danced with happiness. "You made her fertile."

"Many babies. Screaming babies," Esmeralda replied and stroked the end of her long, gray braid. "Babies with stinking diapers."

Cam leaned over and gathered her frail body to him in a hug. "Thank you," he whispered.

She could hardly believe a boy so soft had sprouted from her family tree. It would be a sad day when the world broke him. And Grandmother had a bag full of curses at the ready.

They needed to leave before her benefactor and her nemesis rutted out in the open. The babies wouldn't stop them from mating, but the brats would slow them down. She nudged Cam, who stood transfixed by the couple.

"Closer," she said, "to finish it."

He wheeled her toward the embracing couple. She flicked the ashes in their direction and spoke the final words of the incantation.

As an afterthought, she hurled the plastic ashtray at the devil woman, throwing with little power but true aim. It bounced off of the woman's leg.

Something whacked Kira's ankle. A plastic ashtray with the casino logo lay at her feet. She peeked around Ian to see the old lady who had cursed her, in a wheelchair being pushed by the young man.

Ian looked to see what had captured her attention. To her amazement, he grinned at the pair and gave the woman a little wave. The crone showed teeth more predator than senior citizen and her companion winked. Fear coiled around Kira's heart and squeezed before transforming to anger. How dare they show up when she had one last moment of happiness with Ian? Kira considered chucking the ashtray right back at them.

She stalked up to the young man. "Now look here."

His face scrunched up then he bobbed his head at the elderly woman and waved his hands in a cut-it-off gesture.

"I get it," Kira continued. "Hocus pocus and my life is over." She eyed the crone. "Bad things happen to good people. *Yada yada*."

Ian put his arm around her. "Are you okay?"

"No." She shrugged him off. "I'm not, but I've made peace with it." Squaring her shoulders, she curled her hands into fists, preparing for battle.

If only she had a cross to wave or some holy water to throw on them. If it would save Ian's life, she'd stake the old lady right here, right now, but that probably only worked with vampires.

Ian stared at her, mouth agape. He probably thought she'd lost her mind.

The crone pointed a gnarled finger at her and

muttered something under her breath that sounded like "babies." The hag probably ate them.

"This has all been a misunderstanding. You have nothing to fear from me or my grandmother." The young man glanced at Ian. "Neither of you do."

"If the curse is revoked or whatever, then why the hell did you throw the ashtray at me?" Kira rubbed her foot.

The old woman spat on the carpet.

"Your friend appeased my grandmother, but she's still angry with you," the grandson replied.

Kira's cheeks warmed. If she assaulted or continued yelling at them, all bets were off. She swallowed down the tirade she'd prepared to unleash, refusing to throw away her future after she'd just gotten it back.

"Thank you." She met the crone's eyes and fought against the undertow threatening to drown her in its depths.

"Babies," the old woman said again, ominously.

"You might want to double up on the contraceptives," the young man said. "Just saying." He pushed the wheelchair in the direction of the exit.

Kira took a couple of steps backward and collapsed in a chair. The Stetson pitched forward over her eyes.

"I'm not sure what just happened." Ian adjusted her hat. "What's the deal with the baby thing?"

"A prediction that I'd have lots of children, is my guess."

"She did have the whole creepy, fortune-teller vibe going on. Straight out of a horror movie."

"Definitely scary." With her whole life ahead of her, Kira didn't know what to do first. Of course, she wanted to do Ian, assuming he still wanted to gamble on a relationship with her after all the baby-making comments. The thought of getting pregnant freaked her out, too.

"It seems to me we still have some headway to make on your to-do list. In fact, I think the first order of business should be to add items to the list."

"You're not worried about getting me pregnant?" She touched her abdomen.

"I'd be lying if I said it didn't scare the hell out of me," he admitted, rubbing the back of his neck.

That sounded ominous and final. She lowered her

head. At least she could go home knowing he would be safe. But living without him would be harder than dodging death. The date spent with Ian had ruined her for other guys. Even rock stars. He'd saved her life the moment she'd stepped into his room. *I should find the witch and beg her to finish me off.* She sucked in a breath and tried to work up the energy to smile, her lame attempt at a bluff.

He took her hand and squeezed it to get her attention. "But I'm all in with you."

So much had happened in the space of minutes. Her hopeful brain needed a chance to catch up. She searched his face, her bullshit detector set on high, but found only truth. "Can we make love again before we talk more about having babies?"

"On one condition—before we move on to another item on the list, let's revisit the reverse cowgirl position."

What? "Did I do it wrong?" She couldn't bear the idea of disappointing him in bed.

Ian chuckled. "Not at all. I love the idea of you riding my cock naked, especially when you're wearing the hat."

"Maybe we can take turns wearing it." She ran her finger along the brim.

"That can be arranged," he said, dropping his voice to a whisper. "Let's get the hell out of here before those whack jobs return." He ducked his head and pretended to look around the casino.

"Great idea. Let's swing by the gift shop and pick up more condoms while we're at it. I have a feeling we're going to need them."

"I like the sound of that, darlin'," he said with a Southern twang.

They walked through the casino, hand in hand. She planned to make another bucket list—of all the things she wanted to do with Ian before and after he knocked her up.

Darned curses.

About the Author

Lily Vega lives in the Midwest with her sexy husband who combines all of Dean Winchester's best qualities with a flair for computers. She continually cultivates her dirty mind, fueling it with caffeine and craft beer. She believes all creatures, especially those of the night, deserve mind-blowing sex with a happily ever after.